Disney

GRAPHIC NOVELS #1

PLANES

"Livin' the Dream"

PAPERCUT *Z*

New York

Disney
GRAPHIC NOVELS #1
PLANES

"Livin' the Dream"
Manuscript Adaptation – Alessandro Sisti
(Based on the story by John Lasseter, Klay Hall, and Jeffrey M. Howard
and the screenplay by Jeffrey M. Howard.)
Layout – Roberto Di Salvo, Grafimated, Lucio Leoni
Pencil – Lucio Leoni, Gianfranco Florio, Paco Desiato
Paint – Massimo Rocca, Paco Desiato
Artist Coordination – Tomatofarm
Editorial Pages – Co-d S.r.l. – Milano, Dario Cassani
Pre-Press – Lito Milano S.r.l.
Special Thanks to: Klay Hall, Paul Gerard, Heather Knowles, Jean-Paul Orpinas

DISNEY PUBLISHING WORLDWIDE
Global Magazines, Comics and Partworks

Vice President, Global Magazines and New IP: Gianfranco Cordara
Editorial Director: Guido Frazzini
Editorial Team: Antonella Donola, Virpi Korhonen
Design: Enrico Soave
Art: Caroline LaVelle Egan, Charles E. Pickens
Project Management: Dorothea DePrisco (Director), Mariantonietta Galla, Camilla Vedove
Portfolio Management: Olivia Ciancarelli (Director), Josefina Pierucci

Production – Dawn K. Guzzo
Production Coordinator – Jeff Whitman
Associate Editor – Bethany Bryan
Jim Salicrup
Editor-in-Chief

ISBN: 978-1-62991-286-8 paperback edition
ISBN: 978-1-62991-287-5 hardcover edition

Printed in Canada
August 2015 by Friesens Printing
1 Printer Way
Altona, MB R0G 0B0

FSC
www.fsc.org
MIX
Paper from
responsible sources
FSC® C006398

Papercutz books may be purchased for business or promotional use.
For information on bulk purchases please contact Macmillan Corporate
and Premium Sales Department at (800) 221-7945 x5442.

Distributed by Macmillan
First Papercutz Printing

CONTENTS

PROPWASH JUNCTION

DUSTY

Dusty is a crop duster plane who everyday sprays the fields near Propwash Junction, his home town. But every time he can he practices hard: His dream is to race one day in the Wings Around The Globe Rally together with the best racers in the world.

SKIPPER

Skipper Riley is the old navy plane who teaches Dusty the techniques to fly a little higher. Came to Propwash Junction after the war, he lives a quiet life in town, but this ex top instructor has a secret in his past navy career and Dusty will discover it.

SPARKY

This cheerful and trusty friend of Skipper's has been by his side for many years and he pushes him wherever he needs to go. Sparky is always ready to help in whatever job needs to be done in the hangar.

LEADBOTTOM

Leadbottom is Dusty's boss and he loves his job. While he grumbles about nearly everything in life, he gains enthusiasm when spraying Vita-minamulch on crops. He just doesn't understand Dusty's dreams.

CHUG

Chug is Dusty's best friend and his only supporter in his dream to become a racer. Since Chug has never really travelled outside of Propwash Junction, he's even more engaged in Dusty's journey around the world.

DOTTIE

Together with Chug, this forklift tug runs the Fill 'n' Fly service station. Dottie loves confusing people by using technical language. She's Dusty's mechanic and she knows the limits of his engine; that's why she's a bit worried about his racing.

THE RACERS

RIPSLINGER

He's the most famous racer and the favorite for the upcoming Wings Around The Globe Rally. In the beginning, Rip is Dusty's racing idol, but when the crop duster has the chance to meet him, he sees how arrogant and mean spirited Rip is.

BULLDOG

As the oldest racer of all, he often remembers when GPS wasn't used and planes navigated by stars. He disregards electronic devices and values fairness above all. He has been racing more than the others and he's still among the top.

ROCHELLE

She's the French Canadian champion and has a talent for fast travel. Rochelle is the target of El Chupacabra's constant romantic attentions but she seems to be more focused on winning.

NED & ZED

Ned and Zed are on Ripslinger's team, helping him gain victories and popularity. They are not always smart and sometimes they seem to irritate Rip more than help him.

ISHANI

Followed by over a billion fans, the Indian racer wants to win to make them proud. And thanks to her aerodynamic look and speed, she might be able to. But what is she willing to do to obtain victory?

EL CHUPACABRA

A real superstar in Mexico, El Chupacabra can't pass unnoticed, thanks to his bright presence and his huge engine. Even though the Mexican racer is very different from Dusty, they quickly become friends.

"LIVIN' THE DREAM"
DUSTY CROPHOPPER

NOW LET'S TRY SOME TREE LINE MOGULS.

UH HUH!

ADJUST YOUR ANGLE OF BANK WITH YOUR **ALIEN-IRONS**...

UH?

YOU MEAN **AILERONS**?

OH,... YEAH. RIGHT.

AW, GREAT.

SPUTT

SPUTT

YOU'VE WORN OUT YOUR MAIN BEARING OIL SEAL.

REALLY?

THAT KIND OF DAMAGE COMES FROM **EXTREMELY HIGH SPEEDS**!

BUT YOU'RE A CROP DUSTER AND ALL YOU DO IS DUST CROPS AT **VERY LOW SPEEDS**.

YEP. LOW AND SLOW.

UNLESS YOU'VE BEEN... **RACING AGAIN**!

ME? **NOOO**!

THAT'S **SPEED**! WHERE A SATURN ROCKET COULDN'T CATCH YA, DUSTER!

"...THAT WRAPS UP THE TRY OUTS FOR THE WINGS AROUND THE GLOBE RALLY."

THERE YOU GO! TOPPED OFF AND ALL SET, MAYDAY!

PLEASE, TELL ME THIS IS PROPWASH JUNCTION?

SURE IS!

⌇COUGH!⌇ I'M LOOKING FOR STRUT JETSTREAM!

ME! THAT'S ME!

BUT YOU'RE MISPRONOUNCING IT SLIGHTLY. IT'S ACTUALLY PRONOUNCED...DUSTY CROPHOPPER!

WHATEVER, DUSTY CROPHOPPER... ⌇SNIFF!⌇ WHAT IS THAT SMELL?

IT'S VITA-MINAMULCH...

THE FINEST SMELLING COMPOST THIS SIDE OF THE MISSISSIPPI!

♪ I GOT SOME MINAMULCH, YEAH! ♪

ARE YOU FAMILIAR WITH THE RACING FUEL ADDITIVE NITRO-METHANE?

OH, YEAH, ZIP JUICE! GO-GO PUNCH!

IT'S ILLEGAL!

THAT OL' AIRPLANE NEEDS SOME HELP.

YEAH.

TOTALLY ILLEGAL. YEAH. YOU WERE SAYING?

THAT SUBSTANCE WAS FOUND IN THE TANK OF THE FIFTH PLACE QUALIFIER, FONZARELLI.

24

...UNTIL...

FIREWALL THE THROTTLE!

YOU GOT IT DUSTER!

HE'S READY!

"THERE'S ONE THING MISSING..."

PFSSSSCH

THAT'S COOL!

THE PISTON-AND-CROSSWRENCHES! YOUR SQUADRON *INSIGNIA!*

YOU'VE EARNED IT!

WOOO!

JUST RADIO BACK WHEN YOU GET TO THE CHECKPOINTS.

WE'RE ALL PROUD OF YOU!

SURE WISH YOU WERE COMIN' WITH ME, SKIP.

FLYING INTO **NEW YORK!**

CROPHOPPER 7, TURN FOR THE LEFT HEADING 195. MAINTAIN 1,000 FEET...

BREAK, AIR RACER #7! DO YOU READ KENNEDY APPROACH, OVER?

WHAT...? NEVER MIND! I GOT IT!

UH? I'M DUSTY CROPHOPPER, LOOKIN' FOR **JFK** AIRPORT.

CHECK OUT THIS PAVEMENT! IT'S SO **SMOOTH!**

THUD

25

EXCUSE ME. I'M LOOKING FOR PIT ROW...

YOU MIND? I'M WORKIN' HERE!

STRAIGHT AHEAD AND TO YOUR LEFT.

WELCOME RACERS

OH!

WELL, LOOKIE WHO'S HERE!

YOUR TENT'S THE LAST ONE ON THE LEFT.

THANKS!

WOW! BULLDOG, FROM THE EUROPEAN CUP!

I SAW YOU DO THIS HIGH-G VERTICAL TURN! HOW DID YOU DO THAT?

WHY DON'T I TELL YOU ALL MY RACING SECRETS?

THIS IS A COMPETITION! EVERY PLANE FOR HIMSELF!

YEAH... SURE.

HEY! YOU ARE PAN-ASIAN CHAMPION AND MUMBAI CUP RECORD-HOLDER ISHANI!

MOST PEOPLE JUST CALL ME ISHANI.

I'M DUSTY! I... I MEAN, MY NAME IS DUSTY!

I'M NOT ACTUALLY DUSTY! I'M... QUITE CLEAN.

IT IS VERY NICE TO MEET YOU, QUITE CLEAN DUSTY.

30

YES, BRENT! BULLDOG, THE FLYER FROM THE **UK**, IS IN TREMENDOUS **DANGER!**

IT LOOKS LIKE HE'S FLYING **BLIND!**

I NEED ASSISTANCE! IS ANYONE THERE?

WAIT! IT'S RACER NUMBER 7, CROPHOPPER, PULLING UP BESIDE HIM!

WHAT'S HE DOING?

BULLDOG! APPLY YOUR LEFT AILERON!

OKAY!

STOP ROLL. NOW QUICK PULL UP...

WHOA! **BIG CASTLE!**

VROOOAM

PULL UP, HARD ROLL RIGHT!

ARE YOU STILL THERE?

I'M RIGHT HERE. I'LL FLY RIGHT ALONGSIDE YOU.

AT THE MUNICH AIRPORT...

ACHTUNG! CLEAR THE RUNWAY!

32

ADD POWER... FLAPS DOWN... LANDING GEAR DOWN!

DOWN AND LOCKED!

MUNICH

CHIRP

CHIRP

THANKS FOR YOUR HELP, I...

SPLAAASH

MUNICH

...YOU? WHAT DID I TELL YOU, BOY? EVERY PLANE FOR HIMSELF.

WHERE I COME FROM, IF YOU SEE SOMEONE FALLING FROM THE SKY...

BUT THIS IS A COMPETITION! NOW YOU'RE DEAD LAST... AND I OWE YOU MY LIFE!

BULLDOG!

CAN WE GET A FEW WORDS?

I GOTTA SAY, CROP DUSTER, YOU ARE A NICE GUY.

HEY, THANKS, RIP.

AND WE ALL KNOW WHERE NICE GUYS FINISH... HEH! HEH!

THAT EVENING THE CONTESTANTS RELAX... WELL, NOT ALL OF THEM!

DEAD LAST.

AT LEAST YOU ARE NOT LAST IN THE RACE FOR LOVE.

ROCHELLE?

EXCUSE ME?

MY NAME IS FRANZ AND I AM A HUGE FAN.

I HAVE ...FANS?

JUST ME. I WOULD LIKE TO SAY **DANKE** FOR REPRESENTING ALL US LITTLE PLANES.

BUT YOU ARE A CAR.

JA, BUT I AM A FLUGZEUGAUTO, A **FLYING** CAR!

GUTEN TAG, HERR DUSTY! I AM VO FLIEGENHOSEN!

T-LANK

DIDN'T YOU JUST SAY YOUR NAME IS FRANZ?

FRANZ IS THE GUY WHO IS IN CHARGE WHEN WE PUTTER ABOUT THE COBBLESTONES.

IN THE AIR I AM IN CHARGE!

THIS GUY NEEDS TO GET HIS HEAD GASKET CHECKED...

I HAVE A HUMBLE SUGGESTION. WOULD YOU NOT BE MUCH FASTER WITHOUT THE PIPES AND TANK?

MY SPRAYER?

JA. WHY CARRY AROUND THE EXTR WEIGHT?

THE LITTLE CRAZY CAR IS RIGHT.

IN THE NIGHT...

THIS IS REVERSIBLE, RIGHT?

D-R-RRIIIILLL

FFRRRTCH

THE NEXT DAY...

WOOOH! THANKS FOR EVERYTHING, FRANZ... ER, VON FLIEGENHOSEN!

FANTASTICO!

GUTEN LUCK, HERR DUSTY!

THE RALLY CONTINUES...

IT'S OUR THIRD LEG AND WE'VE ALREADY LOST SEVERAL COMPETITORS TO EQUIPMENT FAILURE.

BUT THE REAL STORY HERE, BRENT, IS DUSTY CROPHOPPER!

AGRA AIRBASE, INDIA...

FROM LAST PLACE, ALL THE WAY TO 8TH!

OH, YEAH!

MISTER RIPSLINGER, HOW CAN A CROP DUSTER OUTFLY YOU?

ONE AT A TIME!

WAIT, WHAT?

THERE HE IS!

DUSTY! DUSTY!

HOW DO YOU KEEP UP WITH THE PROS?

WHY ARE THEY WASTING THEIR TIME WITH HIM?

DUSTY, WHY DO YOU FLY SO LOW?

OH! UH! I...

ACTUALLY, IT'S A REALLY COMPELLING UNDERDOG STORY. IT'S LIKE ROCKY!

IT'S MORE LIKE DAVID AND GOLIATH!

OR OLD YELLER!

ENOUGH!

THAT FARM BOY... HE'S NOT ABOUT TO STOP ME FROM MAKING HISTORY!

WHERE DID YOU LEARN TO RACE?

FROM MY COACH, SKIPPER. HE'S AN AMAZING INSTRUCTOR AND A GREAT FRIEND.

I'M SURE IF HE COULD, HE'D BE RIGHT OUT HERE WITH US.

IF HE COULD...

VRR VRR

RROOARR

YOUR ENGINE SOUNDS KINDA ROUGH.

SPUTT SPUTT

MUST BE A MAG MISFIRE.

THE NEXT MORNING...

YOU GOT ANYTHING NEW?

I'M NOW SELLING THESE ONE-OF-A-KIND DUSTY COMMEMORATIVE MUGS...

AND AFTER ALL THAT SMOKE...

HELLO? IS THIS WHERE I'M SUPPOSED TO BE?

THAT IS ONE OF LIFE'S GREAT QUESTIONS.

⸮GASP!⸮ I'M **DEAD!**

MR. CROPHOPPER. WELCOME TO **NEPAL.**

⸮PHEEEW!⸮ HAVE THE OTHERS LEFT ALREADY?

ACTUALLY, NO ONE ELSE IS HERE YET. YOU'RE IN **FIRST PLACE!**

THAT EVENING...

HE FLEW THROUGH A **WHAT?**

A TUNNEL?

THAT IS **CRAZY!**

SÌ, CRAZY LIKE A FIREFOX!

RIGHT HERE! COME ON!

HOW DOES IT FEEL TO BE IN FIRST PLACE?

IT FEELS GREAT. BUT MORE THAN ANYTHING, I'M HAPPY I FIT THROUGH THAT TUNNEL.

EXCUSE ME, GUYS.

CRAZY DAY TODAY, HUH?

YEAH. A VERY EXCITING WIN FOR YOU.

HEY, YOUR PROPELLER? IT'S NEW, SKYSLICER MARK FIVE, RIGHT?

AREN'T THOSE MADE EXCLUSIVELY FOR **RIPSLINGER'S RACE TEAM?**

DUSTY, I...

I REALLY THOUGHT THAT YOU'D JUST TURN AROUND.

WELL, YOU WERE WRONG. AND I WAS WRONG ABOUT YOU.

OH, HEY, RIP. THANKS FOR FIRST PLACE.

CENTRAL CHINA...

FLYING LOW AND QUICK, DUSTY CROPHOPPER IS MANAGING TO HOLD ON THE TOP SPOT.

BUT CURRENT REIGNING CHAMP RIPSLINGER IS JUST SECONDS BEHIND HIM!

SHANGHAI'S PUDONG INTERNATIONAL AIRPORT...

WE HEAD OUT ACROSS THE PACIFIC TOMORROW, SKIP.

YOU WERE STATIONED THERE FOR A WHILE. GOT ANY ADVICE?

BE CAREFUL.

DURING THE BATTLE OVER WAKE ISLAND, THE WRENCHES RAN INTO SERIOUS MONSOONS!

AND ONE MORE THING...

"THANKS... WINGMAN."

HEY, DUSTY, WE HAVE A SURPRISE FOR YOU!

WE'RE GONNA MEET YOU IN **MEXICO**! TICKETS ARE ON SPARKY AND ME!

WE SOLD 326 DUSTY BOBBLEHEADS, 143 ANTENNA BALLS, 203 SPINNER MUGS...

... AND ONE THOUSAND WHISTL GO TEAM DUSTERINO!

LATER THAT NIGHT...

CLICK

...LOVE MACHINE!!!

NO! NO! NO! A THOUSAND NO'S!

SLAM

≶SOB!≷

QUE PASO? DUSTY, WHAT ARE YOU DOING?

CLICK

LOW AND SLOW.

TCHICA TCHICA

42

JUST A LOVE MACHINE...

AH, SEÑOR EL CHU... YOU'RE PRETTY ROMANTIC FOR A SHOW-OFF!

I AM IN YOUR DEBT, COMPADRE.

COMPADRE. I LIKE THAT.

THE RACE CONTINUES!

NOT TOO BAD FOR A FARM BOY!

SHUMPH!

1 - DUSTY CROPHOPPER   9 - PAC
2 - RIPSLINGER   10 - TYS
3 - NED   11 - SEC
4 - ZED   12 - PIST
5 - EL CHUPACABRA   13 - LITT
6 - BULLDOG   14 - ROD
7 - ISHANI   15 - FIRE
8 - KANEDA

WHAT HAPPENED TO YOU?

THAT SONG... IT FLIPPED A SWITCH!

MY LITTLE MONSTER! COME HERE!

SHE IS LIKE A JAGUAR NOW!

LATER...

THIS IS OUR SIXTH AND LONGEST LEG. THESE RACERS WILL NEED TO FOLLOW THEIR GPS ANTENNAS...

...BECAUSE THERE'S A BIG OCEAN BETWEEN HERE AND MEXICO!

VROOAM

WHANGGG

WHOA!

43

BOGY IS A CIVILIAN. EMERGENCY FUEL.

COPY THAT.

THAT'S ALL I NEED, A CIVILIAN *EXPLODING* ON MY DECK!

WE COULD RIG THE BARRICADE, SIR.

ALL YOU GOTTA DO IS END UP IN THE *SPAGHETTI*.

I'M NOT SURE I CAN DO THIS! THAT RUNWAY IS *MOVING*!

SPROOOOING

WHOOOAAA!

WE GOTCHA CROPHOPPER!

⇒PHEEEW!⇐

HOORAY!

SAFE!

COME ON, LET'S GET YOU FIXED UP, REFUELED AND BACK IN THE RACE.

THANKS, GUYS. YOU SAVED MY TAIL OUT THERE.

HEY, WHAT IS THAT?

THAT'S THE *JOLLY WRENCHES* WALL OF FAME!

EVERY FLYER, EVERY MISSION.

SKIPPER... THERE HE IS! BUT...

45

...WHY'S THERE ONLY **ONE** MISSION?

GLENDAL CANAL

MEANWHILE...

CHUG. WHAT'S ALL THAT?

I'VE NEVER BEEN OUT OF THE COUNTRY. GOTTA BE PREPARED, RIGHT?

SKIPPER?

COME IN, SKIPPER!

DUSTY? WE'RE HEADIN' OFF TO MEXICO RIGHT NOW!

GLAD YA GOT THERE SAFE. WEATHER REPORT SAYS A MAJOR STORM BREWIN' OUT THERE.

I'M NOT IN MEXICO. I'M WITH THE JOLLY WRENCHES.

YOU'RE ON THE FLYSENHOWER?

I SAW THE WALL OF FAME... THEY ONLY LIST ONE MISSION FOR YOU.

IT MUST BE A MISTAKE...

LOOK YOU'VE GOTTA GET OUTTA THERE! YOU'RE GONNA HAVE TO **FLY HIGH**!

IS IT TRUE?

LISTEN TO ME, GET ABOVE THE STORM...

SKIPPER! IS IT **TRUE**?

IT'S TRUE... IT'S TRUE. I ONLY FLEW ONE MISSION.

BUT ALL THOSE STORIES...

CROPHOPPER! WE'VE GOT WEATHER MOVING IN FAST.

ON DECK...

THE CAT WILL TAKE YA FROM ZERO TO 160 KNOTS IN **TWO SECONDS.**

YOU'VE GOT TO TAKE OFF! YOU DON'T GO NOW, YOU DON'T GO **AT ALL.**

ENGINE FULL THROTTLE, NOD TO THE SHOOTER WHEN YOU'RE SET.

GO WIN IT FOR THE WRENCHES, DUSTY! **VOLO PRO VERITAS!**

GO!

CLANK WOOOOSH

MEXICO INTERNATIONAL AIRPORT...

SEÑOR RIPSLINGER, DO YOU HAVE ANY COMMENTS ON THE DISAPPEARANCE OF DUSTY CROPHOPPER?

DUSTY WAS A NICE GUY.

HE FLEW THE CHALLENGE AND PIERCED THE CLOUDS OF MEDIOCRITY. EXCUSE ME.

LET'S HOPE HE MAKES A BETTER BOAT THAN A PLANE.

THAT WAS A GOOD ONE, BOSS.

MALVADOS! SEÑOR DUSTY HAS TEN TIMES THE ENGINE YOU DO!

AND TEN TIMES THE **INTEGRITY!**

SAID THE PLANE WITH THE SHINY NEW PROPELLER...

HOW MUCH INTEGRITY DID THAT ONE COST YOU, SWEETHEART?

OVER THE OCEAN...

HOW CAN IT BE ONLY ONE MISSION?

BA-ROOM

CRAAACK

WHOA!

⸨GASP!⸩

SPUTT SPUTT

SPLAAASH

WRANG

MAYDAY! MAYDAY! I'M GOING DOWN!

18 DEGREES NORTH, 6 MINUTES, 14 SECONDS, 119 POINT...

...HELP!

JUST IN TIME...

QUICK, TO THE HANGAR!

DUSTY!

BROKEN WING RIBS, TWISTED GEAR, BENT PROP AND YOUR MAIN SPAR IS CRACKED...

IT'S OVER.

ONE MISSION? SO MUCH FOR "VOLO PRO VERITAS".

CAN WE GET A MINUTE ALONE, PLEASE?

MY FIRST PATROL AS A JOLLY WRENCH WAS AT GLENDALCANAL.

"MY SQUADRON WAS ALL ROOKIES... I TRAINED EVERY SINGLE ONE OF 'EM..."

LOOK, SKIPPER. ENEMY SHIP, 2 O'CLOCK LOW.

NEGATIVE, JIGSAW 2. OUR ORDERS ARE TO RECON AND REPORT BACK.

COME ON SKIP, IT'LL BE A TURKEY SHOOT!

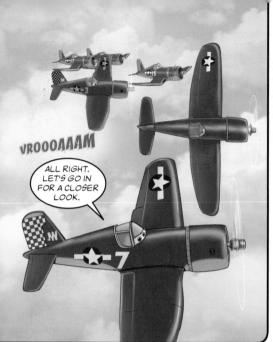

VROOOAAAM

ALL RIGHT. LET'S GO IN FOR A CLOSER LOOK.

"IT WAS TOO LATE TO PULL UP..."

HOLY COW! IT'S THE WHOLE ENEMY FLEET!

⫽AAGH!⫽

BLAM

JIGSAW 2!

RAT-TAT-TAT

⫽UUNGH!⫽

BOOM

AFTER THAT I JUST COULDN'T BRING MYSELF TO FLY AGAIN.

"MY WHOLE SQUADRON... UNDER MY COMMAND... GONE."

IF YOU KNEW THE TRUTH ABOUT MY PAST, WOULD YOU HAVE ASKED ME TO TRAIN YOU?

I'M SORRY, DUSTY.

DUSTY...?

CAN YOU BELIEVE IT? HE HASN'T BEEN STRAIGHT WITH ME THIS WHOLE TIME.

AT LEAST YOU WERE HONEST. YOU SAID I WASN'T BUILT FOR THIS.

IF YOU HAD LISTENED TO ME, I'D NEVER EVER FORGIVE MYSELF.

YOU'RE **NOT** A CROP DUSTER, YOU'RE A **RACER** AND NOW THE WHOLE WORLD KNOWS IT.

THANKS, THAT MEANS A LOT.

I'VE GONE AS FAR I CAN GO. LOOK AT ME...

YES, LOOK AT YOU!

DUSTY, I CANNOT BEAR THE THOUGHT OF COMPETING WITHOUT YOU.

THAT'S THE WING OF A **T-33 SHOOTING STAR!**

EL CHU, I REALLY APPRECIATE...

SILENCIO! YOU HELPED ME WITH MY PURSUITS OF THE HEART.

NOW **WE** ARE HERE TO HELP YOU!

LOOK, HERE'S A **SAT-NAV DEVICE...**

GOT AN EXTRA THRUST REVERSER...

HOW ABOUT A STARTER GENERATOR?

WE?

YES.

HERE'S A **FLOW CONTROL VALVE!**

A NEW PROPELLER? HOW ABOUT A **SKYSLICER MARK FIVE?**

BUT THAT'S **YOUR** PROPELLER! YOU COULD STILL WIN THE RACE!

OH, I INTEND TO...

BUT WITH **MY OLD** PROPELLER. THIS ONE DIDN'T REALLY SUIT ME.

I THINK YOU WILL HAVE A LOT BETTER LUCK WITH IT.

THANKS, ISHANI! DOTTIE, CAN YOU FIX ME?

DOES A **P-T-SIX-A** HAVE A MULTI-STAGE COMPRESSOR?

"YES. **IT DOES!**"

THERE'S A LOT OF WORK TO DO...

... BUT THERE'S ALSO TIME TO **STUDY THE OPPONENT!**

WHEN THE MORNING COMES...

WHOA... DUDE.

WE'LL SEE YOU IN NEW YORK!

HA! IT'S DUSTIN' TIME!

DUSTY!

HE'S BACK!

WHOA, WHO'S THAT GUY?

IT'S THE CROP DUSTER!

ANOTHER ONE?

IS THE SAME ONE, KNUCKLEHEAD!

BOLTING ON A FEW NEW PARTS DOESN'T CHANGE WHO YOU ARE.

YOU'RE AFRAID OF GETTING BEAT BY A CROP DUSTER.

THAT IS WHY THEY CALL 'EM SKYSLYCERS!

SKIPPER, ARE YOU OKAY?

YOU KIDDIN'? I'M GREAT!

GO GET HIM! GO!

OVER THE MISSISSIPPI RIVER...

WE'RE CLOSING IN ON THE FINAL STRETCH, FOLKS!

THAT'S RIGHT, COLIN, AND RIPSLINGER HAS MAINTAINED A FORMIDABLE LEAD!

HI!

WHAT?

⨆ARRGH!⨆ NO, NO, NOOO!

WOOOSH

"TAILWINDS LIKE NOTHING YOU'VE EVER FLOWN..."

ROGER THAT, SKIP!

DON'T LOOK DOWN! DON'T LOOK DOWN!

... A **DUSTER** HAS WON THE WINGS AROUND THE GLOBE RALLY!

"FROM LAST TO FIRST, FROM OBSCURITY TO IMMORTALITY, THE RACING WORLD WILL NEVER FORGET THIS DAY! FOR THE FIRST TIME..."

A-HAAA! **NUMERO UNOOO!**

YOU REALLY LICKED HIS BOTTOM, LAD!

YOU DID IT!

I COULDN'T HAVE DONE IT WITHOUT YOU, DOTTIE.

YEAH, I KNOW.

THE WORLD HAS A NEW CHAMPION ...AND SO DO I.

AWESOME, DUSTY!

GREAT TIP ABOUT RIPSLINGER LEANING TO THE CAMERAS! THANKS, CHUG!

HEY, ANYTHING FOR MY PAL.

THANKS, ISHANI. FOR EVERYTHING.

)WHEW!(**RIPSTINKER!** YOU NEED TO GO HOME AND WASH UP... **TWICE!**

)GRRR!(

WHO'S THAT GUY?

UH?

THE END

WATCH OUT FOR PAPERCUT

Welcome to the high-flying premiere of DISNEY GRAPHIC NOVELS, a brand-new series from Papercutz, those crazy young men and women in their flying machines, dedicated to publishing graphic novels for all ages! Papercutz is also the very same publisher who has been bringing you the adventures of Tinker Bell and all her fairy friends in the DISNEY FAIRIES graphic novel series for the past few years! I should know, I'm Jim Salicrup, the Editor-in-Chief of Papercutz—which considering just these two titles is a little like being an air traffic controller!

But unlike DISNEY FAIRIES, which features Tinker Bell and all her fairy friends from Pixie Hollow in each and every graphic novel, DISNEY GRAPHIC NOVELS will be featuring a rotating line-up of awesome Disney super-stars! Starring in our premiere volume, is DISNEY PLANES, those amazing air aces we all know and love. But coming your way in the very next volume of DISNEY GRAPHIC NOVELS will be none other than the character who is virtually synonymous with Disney—Mickey Mouse himself! He's starring in an all-new series where he confronts and explores the supernatural in a way that only he can! It's Mickey Mouse as you've never seen him before battling ghosts and goblins in a full-length graphic novel adventure! It's called X-MICKEY, and we're sure you're going to love it!

Then coming up in the thrilling third volume of DISNEY GRAPHIC NOVELS will be a collection of fun and fashionable stories starring Minnie Mouse and Daisy Duck!

These two wonderful BFF are having all sorts of exciting times together and now you'll be able to frolic with them as well.

We're going to keep it a secret for now as to exactly what awaits you in DISNEY GRAPHIC NOVELS #4, but we will say it's nothing that you'll ever suspect! But we will tell you that in DISNEY GRAPHIC NOVELS #5, DISNEY PLANES returns with all-new stories starring Dusty Crophopper and his friends.

Way back in the very first DISNEY FAIRIES graphic novel I told you how thrilled I was to be working on Disney comics—that it was a dream come true. Now that we've added DISNEY GRAPHIC NOVELS I'm even more thrilled! When Papercutz publisher Terry Nantier and I first founded Papercutz, we could only dream about possibly publishing gaphic novels featuring comics from Disney. After all, we wanted to bring everyone the very best comics for all ages that we possibly could—and what could possibly be better than Disney?

Yet the most important thing is what you think! So please let us know—either write us a letter and mail it to the address below or send us an email! After all, we're doing all this for you. Let us know what you like and/or what you don't like. Then we'll do everything we possibly can to make DISNEY GRAPHIC NOVELS the very best comicbook experience possible for you!

Off we go!

STAY IN TOUCH!

EMAIL: salicrup@papercutz.com
WEB: www.papercutz.com
TWITTER: @papercutzgn
FACEBOOK: PAPERCUTZGRAPHICNOVELS
REGULAR MAIL: Papercutz, 160 Broadway, Suite 700, East Wing, New York, NY 10038

Don't miss DISNEY GRAPHIC NOVELS #2 "X-Mickey"—Coming Soon!